CHET series

From Out of Nowhere

Whispers From the Past

Strength Beyond Our Own

Hidden in the Heart

CHET

From Out of Nowhere

Larry Murray

This is a work of fiction. All of the characters and events portrayed in this novel are either products of the author's imagination or are used fictitiously.

Published by

Sandy Cedars Publishing

791 E 1550 N

Shelley, Idaho 83274

ISBN 978-1943632015

To Jackie

My first reader outside the family and my most vocal fan.

Thank you

Chapter 1

April 13, 1964

The blue and white Homelite chainsaw screamed and shuddered as Charles made the undercut on the ancient juniper. He worked the plunger on the manual oiler to keep the chain lubricated, each squirt spawning a cloud of blue smoke that rose from the bar. When he had sunk the cut half way through the trunk, he backed the saw out and allowed the engine to drop to a rumbling idle. Wiping saw chips from his face, he sized up the angle required to complete the notch. He positioned the saw, revved the engine and proceeded with the diagonal cut.

Charles stepped back from the tree, straightening, he arched his back to ease his aching muscles. He was working on felling the fourth tree of the morning and there were still three to go in order to clear the fence line for his expanded corral. Charles oriented the bar horizontally, a couple of inches above the initial undercut. He revved the saw and fed the spinning teeth into the trunk, making the felling cut. The big tree shuddered and popped, the sound clear even above the noise of the racing saw.

Charles backed quickly away and the sixty-foot tree seemed to hang suspended for a few moments before gravity took hold and it arced towards the ground with a crashing thump. Branches splintered and flipped, spinning into the air, accompanied by a stifling cloud of dust which lingered in the air long after the tree was stilled.

A movement caught his eye and Charles looked across the nearly empty stack yard to see his wife and young son approaching. He killed the saw and tucked it below the curve of the three-foot-diameter trunk of the tree he had just felled, safely away from the inquisitive explorations of his four-and-a-half-year-old son, Jason. He stripped off his hearing protection and waved.

Jason returned the wave and with a grin he broke free from Emily and raced across the ground, squealing a greeting as he came. Charles squatted down and Jason charged into his arms, nearly bowling him over.

"Whatcha doing, Dad? Can I help?"

Charles rose, giving his son a hug. "I'm cutting down trees to make room for a bigger corral."

"How come?"

"The corral is too small for the stock we have and we still have too few cows to make a proper dairy for Tucker and Son."

Jason scrunched his face in concentration. "How many cows do we have?"

"By the time the last of the springers calve, and I cull ten of the oldest cows, we'll have forty head in the milking herd."

"That's a lot," Jason pronounced soberly.

"It is a lot, and it has taken eight years and a lot of hard work to get here. Like we've talked about, we're going to build our herd to eighty head before we level off."

"How long will that take?"

"Another four or five years, depending on how many calves are heifers and how many cows we have to cull between now and then."

Jason scowled. "What's cull?"

"Cull means the cow has gotten too old to give enough milk. When that happens we take her to the auction and sell her to someone else. Someone who doesn't need her milk like we do."

At that moment Emily arrived, distracting Jason from the followup question that would have otherwise led to the inevitable discussion on butchering and making hamburger. Charles wrapped his free arm around his wife and gave her a kiss on the forehead.

Emily looked up at her husband, squinting against the sun. "It sounds like you're still filling his head with dreams of a family dairy. What if he grows up and decides he wants to marry a city girl?"

Charles snorted a laugh. "Not much chance of that happening when he lives in rural Idaho, but even if it does, it's OK. At least it is as long as she's willing to settle down on the farm and help with the milking and feeding."

Emily squeezed his hand. "Just don't get so set on your dream that there's no room for Jason to have dreams of his own."

Charles shrugged uncomfortably as the conversation headed into territory it had traveled all too frequently over the past year or two. *I don't think it would have ever become an issue if Jason had been joined by brothers and sisters like we'd always planned, but something changed when Emily learned we'll never have any more children. I think she has come to terms with it, but she's adamant that I leave Jason's choices open to whatever he wants to do with his life. I'm OK with that, but I still don't see any problem with treating his future as if it's conforming to my plans. If he doesn't like it, he can always tell me he wants to do something else.*

"I'm sure you and Jason didn't come all the way out to the stack yard just to remind me there are occupations other than dairy farming."

"No, we didn't." Emily smiled, hefting the basket slung from her arm. "We came bearing lunch. I figure this way you'll get something to eat and Jason will wear himself out a bit so he'll be ready to take his nap when he's supposed to."

"Well, I don't know about you two, but lunch sounds pretty good at the moment. That four o'clock breakfast wore off some time ago." Charles gestured to the fallen tree. "Why don't you have yourself a seat and we'll see what you've got hidden in your basket."

Emily seated herself and Charles sat down beside her, balancing Jason on his knee.

Emily pulled the cloth back and the smell of fried chicken wafted from the basket. There were rolls, potato salad, and a quart jar of lemonade to go with the chicken. Emily handed plates to Charles and Jason and placed the third on her lap. She dished up servings for each of them and raised her eyebrows when Charles started looking for utensils.

"What about the blessing, Charles?"

"Oh, you're right. Guess it kind of slipped my mind with it being a picnic and all." He turned to his son. "Would you like to fold your arms and ask the blessing for us?"

Jason nodded, holding his plate out for his father to hold so he could fold his chubby arms. He bowed his head and raced through the prayer, blessing the food and Mommy and Daddy and the cows and the birds and the sunshine. When he brought the prayer to a close, Charles and Emily echoed his exuberant amen.

Charles started with the chicken breast. Smacking his lips, he grinned at his wife. "I can't begin to list all the reasons it was a good idea to marry you, but your cooking has to be right up there at the top of the list."

"I appreciate the compliment, Charles, but I hope our marriage has a stronger foundation than my cooking."

"Oh, believe me, it does."

"Like what exactly?"

Charles tipped his cap back and scratched his head. "Well, let's see. You're a darn good driver. I can't think of anyone I'd rather have in the truck when we're rolling up and down the field hauling hay." Charles flashed a mischievous smile. "You're also a great calf-feeder, not to mention chicken-tender. Not only that, you grow a mean garden. Tomatoes, Swiss chard, carrots, and my favorite, sweetcorn."

Emily shook her head. "That sounds like I'm a maid or a hired hand. Is that all you see in our marriage?"

Charles shrugged. "Pretty much, other than the fact that you're the best wife a man could ever hope for and you're doing a wonderful job raising our son. With your influence there's a better than even chance that he won't turn out to be a complete heathen like his dad."

Emily smiled. "You're not a complete heathen, Charles."

Charles snorted a laugh. "Not a *complete* heathen, huh? Just mostly ..."

"That's not what I meant and you know it. You've still got a few rough edges, but you clean up pretty well."

"But?" Charles prompted as the silence began to drag out.

"I don't know. It just seems like we don't get away to do much anymore."

"That's kind of what you signed up for, my dear. Milking is a twice-a-day, three-hundred-and-sixty-five-days-a-year proposition. Throw in growing our own feed and there's not a lot of time for getting away."

"I know that, Charles. It's just that I don't want us to go through life without making any memories. I don't want us to be sitting in our rocking chairs in fifty years and looking back with regret that our life together was nothing but work."

"It's not all work. We've got Jason here, and you're always going out of your way to do special things like this picnic lunch. Besides that, we go to church as a family every Sunday and you're singing in the choir and teaching in the Sunday school. What more could you ask for in the way of diversion?"

Emily shook her head. "Sounds like more work to me."

"Maybe." Charles shrugged. "But it also sounds a lot like building memories and spending time together. Besides, in the winter we play Monopoly as often as I can talk you into it."

Emily fixed him with a fierce glare. "If you wouldn't beat me all the time I might be more willing to play more often. I think you cheat."

"I don't cheat. You're the one who agrees to the property swaps I propose."

"Maybe I need to say no more often."

"That all depends on what you're saying no to. If we're still talking about Monopoly, maybe you should. It would most likely make the game more interesting."

Emily sighed. "Is that what you're doing, Charles? Are we building our own real-life version of Monopoly? Buying land and improving it?"

"I'm not sure where all this is coming from, Emily. You know what our plan is, and that we're well on our way to making it a reality. What's wrong?"

"I don't know. I guess I've just been thinking lately about how our plans have a way of changing on us." Her gaze shifted to Jason, who was busy stuffing his mouth with chicken and dinner rolls. Her hand strayed to her belly and her eyes lifted, seeking Charles' eyes. "You're always telling me that things will be better next year. I'm not complaining, but I guess I'm wondering if next year is ever going to come."

"Funny you should mention that." Charles gave Emily a small, crooked smile. "With over a hundred and thirty head of stock on the place, our corral is too small. Hence the expansion project I've been working on this spring. We've got our new barn up and it's more than adequate for running seventy or even eighty head of cows. I figure we'll be up to those numbers in another four, maybe five years. In the meantime, I've decided we need to cut back on raising steers. We don't really have the room at the moment, and even if we did I think we'd be better off putting the feed into the heifers. In a few years we're going to be raising more springers than we'll need as replacements. We'll keep the best ones and sell the rest. It'll be nice to be on the other side of the springer market for a change."

"So what are you going to do with all the steers?"

"The nineteen head of yearlings will go to auction as normal over the next few weeks. The change is that I think we need to get rid of the ten younger steers as well. As the bull calves come along we'll get them up to weaning age and sell them to some of our neighbors who are looking for light feeders."

"I think it's wonderful that you're getting rid of some of the stock, but won't you need the money from the sale to pay for the expansion of the corral?"

"Some of it," Charles acknowledged. "But the fact is I've been thinking it's time to upgrade our loader tractor. That old tricycle Farmall is just too dangerous for an inexperienced driver and it won't be all that long before Jason will be ready to start helping with the tractor work."

"Really, Charles? Every time you get on that tractor to haul manure I'm scared to death. Ever since you tipped it over in the swale last fall I just know you're going to do it again and next time we won't be so lucky."

"I know you've been scared, and that's why I've been looking. I've got my eye on a used Massey that should work out just fine. It's got a wide front end so there'll be no more tipping under load."

"Will there be enough money to build the corral and replace the tractor both?"

Charles shrugged. "That all depends. If we get a decent price out of the steers, and if they give us a reasonable trade-in for the Farmall, we should be OK." Charles pushed his cap back and scratched his head. "In fact, if I've got things figured right, we may just have enough to get that pickup we've been wishing for."

"Really?" Emily's face lit with a smile. "Does that mean you'd quit using the car for irrigating and parts runs to town?"

Charles laughed at his wife's little-girl enthusiasm. "With everything you do for me and our son, the least I can do is give you a car you don't have to vacuum and wash before you feel it's clean enough to take to church."

Emily blushed. "It's not just that. I think it's past time that you retire Brutus, at least for running back and forth to town or irrigating on those rare occasions I've got the car."

Charles smiled. "I know Brutus embarrasses you, but I honestly don't mind driving him."

Emily's eyebrows rose.

Charles shrugged. "You're right, I don't mind driving him *that* much. He is pretty unwieldy, and it is kind of ugly the way the cows redecorate the stock rack every time I take a load to the auction. Otherwise, it's not *too* embarrassing."

Emily giggled. "I'm all about saving you from embarrassment, but promise me one thing. Your pride is less important than your safety, so don't spend so much on a pickup that you can't afford to replace the Farmall."

"I won't," Charles promised.

"In that case"—Emily smiled as she slipped her hand into the basket—"I think my men have been good enough that they've earned a treat." She pulled out a small plate of homemade chocolate-chip cookies.

Jason squealed and Charles grinned, nodding his head vigorously. "We've been very good. Haven't we, Jason?"

The little boy's cheeks puffed out like a chipmunk as he forced an oversized bite into his mouth.

Charles felt a tug at his heart as he looked at his greasy-faced only child. *Emily's right. As important as work is, I can't afford to let life pass me by without spending time with my wife and child. I'm never going to get another chance at seeing my child grow up.*

A persistent poking in his chest brought Charles out of his reverie. He glanced down at the chocolate-covered finger that was poking him in the ribs. "What, Jason?"

"Can I have a piece of the tree?"

"A piece of the tree? I guess so. There are plenty of branches. I could cut you a walking stick if you'd like."

"No, Dad. I want a big piece."

"A big piece? What are you going to do with it?"

Jason shrugged. "Something."

"Something? Like what?" Charles looked at Emily for direction on how he should respond to their son's request.

Emily shrugged as Jason slid off his dad's lap.

Jason walked to the end of the trunk and took a deep breath. "I like the smell."

"A walking stick will smell just as good," Charles assured him.

Jason shook his head. "No. I need a big piece!"

"How big?"

Jason stretched out his arms, marking off a twelve-inch length.

"I don't know," Charles murmured. "That seems like a pretty big piece."

Jason's face split in a grin as he stretched his arms even further.

Charles bent down and brought his face next to his son's face. "What in the world are you going to do with an eighteen-inch section of a tree trunk?"

"I'm going to use it as a chair next time we have a picnic."

Emily giggled and Charles fixed her with a glare.

"Oh, come on, Charles. Be a sport. It won't cost you anything but a few minutes of your time to cut him off a section of the trunk. You're just going to cut the tree up and burn it as firewood anyway. What would it hurt to give him a chair?"

"If I do, you're the one who's going to have to deal with the sap-oozing mess. I don't know how you'd ever get it off his clothes."

Emily raised her hand to hide her smile as Charles turned to his son.

"I'll tell you what. I'll cut you a block for a chair on one condition. We have to put it in the shop until it dries. Once it's dry we'll figure out together how to make it into a chair for you. Deal?"

Jason jumped up and down, clapping his hands and squealing in delight.

"What do you tell your dad, Jason?"

"Thank you, Daddy!"

Calvin Ellis approached the door bearing a metal plate with 'Sales Manager' engraved across its surface. He knocked on the doorframe and poked his head into the office. "You wanted to see me, boss?"

Alan Wright looked up from the ledger and beckoned to his subordinate. "Yes, Cal. Please come in and close the door."

Alarms started going off in Cal's head as he pulled the door closed and seated himself in one of the two chairs pulled up in front of the sales manager's desk. Unlike his own modest cubbyhole, this entire office was designed to convey a sense of the power and authority wielded by its occupant. From the massive wood desk and rich wood paneling on the walls, to the plush carpet on the floor, it all served to put him on notice that he was in his boss's territory.

Cal cleared his throat. "How can I help you, Al?"

Alan shook his head, a breathy sigh escaping through his teeth. "I've been going through the books, Cal, and I have to tell you I'm not pleased with what I see. I stuck my neck way out for you last September when we ordered in that orange and white Chevy C-10 for

Thompson Plumbing. We decked that thing out especially for them, and you assured me it was a solid deal. Here we are six months after it was delivered and it's still sitting on the lot and clogging up my books."

"How was I supposed to know that Bob Thompson was going to have a heart attack that would put him out of commission for months if not permanently? I've checked in with him regularly and at this point it's anyone's guess whether or not he'll lose his business and possibly his home."

"Not my problem, Cal." Alan twirled his expensive gold pen, its shape blurring as it snapped back and forth in his fingers. "What is my problem is getting rid of that truck before the owner decides I'm not doing my job." The pen stopped spinning and he thrust it in Cal's direction. "I'm not going to be pleased if the boss comes down on me for bringing in a truck that you've failed to move."

"I understand what you're saying, Al. What kind of flexibility do I have?"

The smile that parted Alan's lips would have made a shark envious.

"You have all the flexibility in the world, Cal, at least as long as it comes from your side of the sale. After six months of carrying dead inventory, the dealership has already contributed everything it's going to give up. Furthermore, since you've already had more than enough time to move a single vehicle, I can only assume you lack motivation. That being the case, consider this your notice that thirty days from now either that truck is gone or you are." Alan smiled again. "It's entirely up to you."

Cal bit down on the response he wanted to make and instead nodded, rose from the chair and walked from the room. When he had moved out of sight of the open doorway he sagged against the wall. *Of all the arrogant, egotistical wastes of skin to ever walk the earth! I can't believe he's pulling crap like that. Punishing me for failing to make a sale because the customer has a heart attack and nearly dies.*

Cal pushed himself away from the wall and headed for the door leading to the lot. *I shouldn't be surprised. The fact that I've worked here for twenty-two years and am grandfathered in at two percent above everyone else's commission has never sat well with him. It looks like he has finally found the pretext he needs to fire me. On the other hand, I've still got thirty days to unload a specially equipped pickup to someone who hasn't a clue that it's exactly what they need.*

Chapter 2

Charles idled Brutus back towards the loading chute, his foot hovering over the clutch, his eyes focused intently on Emily as she guided him back. She crossed her forearms at the same moment her clear soprano called out for him to stop. He mashed the clutch and brake pedals to the floor and watched for a few moments to give his wife time to confirm the position of the truck. She nodded and he turned the key, silencing the engine.

He turned to his son, who was sharing the cab, both because he loved to ride in the oversized truck with his dad and to keep him out from underfoot as Charles and Emily loaded the cattle for the auction. "Jason, I need you to be a big boy. Your mom and I have to load some steers so I can take them to the auction. Can you sit quiet so you don't scare the cattle?"

"Can I watch through the back window?"

"As long as you don't move around or make any noise. Daddy won't be happy if you scare the steers and they come back out of the truck and run over him."

Jason laughed as he repeated the mantra Charles had drilled into him over the past several years that he had been visiting the barn and corrals. "The cows are more scared of you than you are of them."

"That's true, Jason, but if they see you through the window it could startle them and they really would come right back out of the truck. That's why it's so important for you to be a big boy. No moving and no noises. Can you do that for me?"

Jason nodded solemnly.

"Good boy. Now I better get back there or your mother is going to be wondering what's happened to me." Charles slid off the seat, stepping onto the running board and then down to the ground. He retrieved his whip from behind the seat, waved at his young son, and closed the door.

Never one to slack off, Emily had heaved the sliding door up and had secured the rope with a single figure-eight around the cleat.

Charles shook his head as he considered his wife, standing beside the ungainly farm truck. The truck was a 1950 Chevy 6400 two-ton. It was painted army green and mounted a metal-plated flat bed with pockets for stakes. Hidden below the bed was a massive ram that had allowed it to dump whatever loads its original owner had dictated that it carry during the first eight years of its life. Charles had purchased it shortly after he bought the farm, and had converted the metal-sparred, wooden-sided dump bed into a cattle rack. It wasn't pretty, but it was serviceable, at least for hauling heavy loads, as long as one wasn't forced to park in too tight a space or next to neighbors who were too refined.

"What are you smiling about?" Emily asked, a small smile parting her own lips.

"I was just thinking that I jumped the gun in naming this truck Brutus." Charles wrapped his wife in an embrace. "If I'd waited until after we were married, I'd have christened him the Beast."

Emily raised her eyebrows.

Charles chuckled at her familiar mannerism. "As in Beauty and the Beast." Charles grinned and moved in for a kiss.

Emily returned his kiss then abruptly pushed against his chest. "Charles Tucker, you smell like a barnyard!"

"After a morning of milking I'm not surprised, but then you shouldn't be either. You had a pretty good idea who I was and what I smelled like before you ever agreed to marry me."

"True, but you used a different aftershave when we were dating."

"Same aftershave. I just always made sure I bathed before I ventured too close."

"Ah-ha! You just admitted your deceitful tactics. I clearly didn't know what you smelled like before we said 'I do.'"

"Good try, my dear, but I happen to know how smart you are and there's no way such a shallow deception would have worked on you."

"Maybe I mistakenly believed I'd always be important enough to you that you'd clean up before you tried to kiss me."

"Oh, you're important enough, but if I had to bathe before I could kiss you we'd never share even half as many kisses as we do."

"Perish the thought." Emily smiled and gave him a quick kiss. She inclined her head towards the truck. "At the moment, however, we have an audience and we need to get these steers loaded or you'll get them to the auction so late you'll miss out on half the buyers."

Charles sighed. "Even though you *are* a taskmaster, you've still got a point. I'll be a good boy and get the steers loaded if you'll keep an eye on the rugrat."

"Charles Tucker, that's no way to talk about your son."

"That's probably true. Although all things considered, he does tend to fall into disfavor when he insists on interrupting my fun."

Emily shook her head, color creeping into her cheeks. "There will be no more fun until you get those steers loaded, taken to the auction and sold, put in an honest day's work and have had your nightly bath."

"You drive a hard bargain, but since that's what I already had in mind I'll agree to your terms."

"Of course. It would never do to let me think that I had any influence on your decisions."

Charles snorted a laugh. "At least no more influence than you already think you have." *Since there's absolutely nothing I wouldn't do for you, the least you can do for me is to leave me with the dignity of believing I have some choice in the matter.* He snapped the whip and it responded with a rifle-shot pop. "Now that that's settled, I'll see what I can do to persuade the steers to get in the truck."

Charles squinted as he walked out of the auction and into the bright afternoon sunlight. He adjusted his cap and stumped across the parking area to where Brutus sat. *Well, that was a fine howdy-do! I started bringing my stock here to Blackfoot because I felt like they did a better job than the auction in Idaho Falls. After today, I'm not so sure. I may not be a big part of their business but I deserve to be treated better than that.*

Arriving at the truck, he climbed inside and pulled the door sharply, slamming it much harder than was necessary. *It's been a while since I last sold any cattle, but it sure looked like those two buyers were in cahoots. I can spot 'em a mile off. They always wear cowboy hats while we farmers tend to wear caps. I suspect some of the cowboy hat wearers are actually ranchers, but I've got a feeling those two fellers were professional buyers. Why else would the auction have split my five head into two groups rather than running them as one?*

Charles stuffed the key into the ignition and turned it to the run position. He stomped on the starter button on the floor and Brutus' engine turned over a few times before it caught and smoothed out. *I may be jumping to conclusions that they were taking turns buying so they could shave a few cents off, but it really burns me that one of my steers was hurt on the way to the ring. He was fine when I unloaded him but he was definitely limping when he came through the ring. That limp cost me three cents a pound and it wasn't just on the injured steer, it was on all three in the group.*

Looking both ways, Charles gunned the truck and pulled onto the road fronting the livestock auction. *I can't believe the old hag in the office had the gall to try to tell me my steer was probably roughed up by someone else's cattle. I wasn't born yesterday. I'd bet dollars to nickels that some impatient handler pushed him on slick footing and he went down. I guess I should consider myself lucky that he didn't break a leg. Especially since it's not all that lucky to have them cost me seventy-five to eighty bucks right off the top of three prime steers. That's money I need to feed my family and pay the mortgage on the farm and my new barn. For that matter, it could make all the difference on whether or not I can actually afford to get a pickup so I can quit driving this oversized monster around town.*

Charles crossed the tracks and braked to a stop at the Yellowstone Highway. When the traffic opened up, he pulled onto the highway and headed towards downtown Blackfoot. *In spite of the skinning I just took, I still might as well check out that used pickup I saw advertised in the paper. If I get a decent price on the rest of the cattle I should still be able to swing sixteen hundred for a three-to four-year-old pickup.*

Wrestling the truck through the downtown traffic that spilled over onto the highway, Charles made his way to Judicial Street and turned into its even narrower confines. He made his way to Modern Motor and turned into an open area near the back of their lot. *Well that was a load of fun. Now the only thing that could make things better would be to find out that the truck is already sold and that I've got to back Brutus onto the street because there's no way to wangle my way around so I can pull out going forwards.*

He released a grim chuckle and mentally shook himself, doing his best to banish the dark feelings that had stalked him for the past hour. *Charles, old boy, Emily would be downright disappointed in the way you've been acting. She'd tell you to man up, and that I have no right to spread my gloom and anger on another human being. She'd be right too, so buck up and at least act like a civilized man.*

Climbing down from Brutus' cab, Charles set off across the lot to where he could see the pickups lined up in neat rows. *That seems like as good a place to start as any.* He was halfway down the second row when he looked up and saw an older gentleman approaching. His dress slacks and tie indicated he was a salesman rather than another buyer checking out the vehicles on the lot. *Just my luck, he's old enough to be my father. No matter how much Emily would undoubtedly tell me to be patient, I'm not in the mood to listen to an old man's stories for the next two hours.*

The salesman was two inches shorter than his own five-foot-ten-inch height, enabling Charles to clearly see the balding patch that started in the front and disappeared somewhere beyond the crown of his head. He wore black-rimmed glasses, and his face and belly were both rounded by the two hundred pounds packed onto his frame.

He extended his hand with a smile. "Good afternoon. I'm Cal Ellis. How can I help you on this beautiful spring afternoon?"

Charles accepted his hand and returned his surprisingly firm grip. "Charles Tucker. I saw an ad in the *Shelley Pioneer* on a '61 Chevy pickup you have for sale. I recall the asking price being fifteen-hundred and eighty-nine dollars. If it looks to be in good enough shape I thought I might take it for a test drive."

"Well, you're in luck, Charles. We've still got the '61 pickup and I'd be delighted to show it to you." He gestured back toward where Brutus was parked. "Our used pickups are back that way. While we're walking, why don't you tell me a bit about yourself and what you want your pickup to do for you?"

Charles shrugged. *If we have to talk, I guess talking about myself beats listening to you talk about yourself.*

"You said you saw our ad in the *Pioneer*. You have a farm up near Shelley?"

Charles nodded. "I have a place north of Shelley. I run a herd of Grade A milk cows."

"Really? How many head?"

"About forty head at the moment, but I'm building the herd to eighty head."

"Sounds like an awful lot of work to me."

"It is that." Charles smiled, relaxing in spite of himself.

"So are you looking for a truck to kick around the farm? Make a few trips to town?"

"Pretty much." Charles nodded. "I need something to haul parts and supplies, do the irrigating, in general to keep the farm out of my wife's car."

"So you're not replacing an existing truck?"

"Nope. I'm looking to make a cash deal so I'm after the best price you can give me."

Cal smiled. "Before we worry too much about the price, let's find out if the used truck will fit your needs. If not, we've got plenty of other options we can explore. One way or the other I'm sure we've got exactly what you need."

"What I need is going to have to take second place to what I can afford to spend."

"Don't worry, Charles. I'll work with you on the price. We're a small-town dealer, so we don't have the overhead the guys in Idaho Falls do. I'm sure we can come together on the price."

Cal led them to a green and white pickup parked near the back of the lot. There were some older, more severely used and beat-up trucks on the back row, but it was clear what the dealership thought of the status of this particular truck. Cal opened the door, pulled down the visor, and deftly caught the keys that fell out. "Would you like to take a look at its condition first, or would you rather start it up?"

"How about we check it out first?"

"Good idea." Cal gestured to the front of the truck. "Let's start with the engine." He raised the hood and stepped to the side so Charles had an unobstructed view. "She's got a 283 V8 engine, which is a perfect match for the three-quarter-ton chassis. The four-speed transmission gives you a wide range of ground speeds. At thirty-five thousand miles she has covered a lot of ground, but you can see her engine is still good and tight."

Cal gestured for Charles to precede him. "The body is in good shape. It's a one-owner truck that was used in construction so a lot of the miles are highway miles. It's also the reason for it being a three-quarter-ton. Heavy loads, if you know what I mean."

Charles nodded, taking in every detail as they walked around the truck. There were a few scrapes and dings but nothing too severe and there was no serious rust. The bed was in fairly good shape except for a deep gouge in one board that lined up with a matching crease on the inside of the tailgate. "Looks like they hauled something pretty heavy that was more than a little reluctant to slide out of the bed."

"Looks like it." Cal shrugged. "Still, all in all it's in pretty good shape for a work truck. The original owner used up maybe a third of its life, but it's priced at little more than half the cost of a new truck."

"True, and for knocking around I don't mind living with someone else's dings and scrapes. But if I were looking for a knock-around truck we'd be looking at those." Charles jerked a thumb at the pickups one row further back on the lot.

"Come now, Charles, you're already trying to dicker me down and you haven't even heard her run yet. At least sit in her and start her up before you start worrying about the price." Cal grinned and jingled the keys before dropping them into Charles' hand.

Charles nodded and slid into the driver's seat. He fit the key into the ignition and started cranking the engine.

"You may have to give her a bit of choke," Cal coached.

Charles pulled the choke partway out and the engine caught immediately, growling to life with a muted roar. He eased off on the choke and the accelerator and the V8 settled into a low rumble. He flexed the gas pedal a couple of times and the engine revved smoothly, rocking the pickup side to side in response to the torque of the big engine. Charles' face split into a grin. *The suspension and the engine to handle a big load. She may not be able to carry what Brutus will, but she'll be far more agile and easier to drive in town, not to mention irrigating and everything else I have to do on the farm.*

Charles pushed buttons and pulled levers, checking to confirm that everything worked. The heater fan was a bit noisy but otherwise everything checked out, from the windshield wipers to the radio. As the engine warmed up, Charles released the choke and the engine settled into a muted rumble.

Raising his voice to be heard, he addressed Cal. "How about letting me take it for a test drive?"

"Sure. We just need to pull over to the showroom so I can pick up a set of dealer plates. There are some forms to sign if you want to take it by yourself, or we can circumvent all the tomfoolery by having me ride along."

Charles shrugged. "Makes no difference to me. If you want to ride along I'm sure I can still learn what I need to know about the truck."

"Sounds good. Hang on while I climb in and you can pull around to the south side door and I'll grab the plates. We'll be on our way in a few minutes."

Forty-five minutes later, Charles downshifted and nosed the pickup into the Modern Motor lot. "Where would you like me to park it?"

"That all depends on what you think of her. If you're ready to go ahead we can pull in right up front here and we'll take care of the paperwork."

"Slow down there." Charles raised his hands from the wheel in a warding gesture. "I'm not that certain that I'm ready to commit."

"No problem. Like I said, we've got lots of options and I want to make sure you're going to be happy with your decision. I've been at this game for a lot of years and I'm all about repeat customers." Cal grinned and gestured toward the back of the lot. "Let's go ahead and take her back where we found her, and while we're doing that, why don't you tell me what's bothering you about her?"

Charles shrugged. "There's nothing really big. It seems solid and the engine sounds good."

"But?" Cal prompted.

"I don't know. I guess I'm a little surprised at the gearing. Other than its size it doesn't drive all that differently than Brutus over there." In response to Cal's questioning look, Charles gestured at the green cattle truck. "Third gear was OK for around town, but first and second were pretty much a waste. It felt like I was racing the engine to keep up with the flow of traffic. On the highway, it didn't settle down until I hit fourth. I guess I expected a broader response from a pickup, especially one as nearly new as this one is."

Cal nodded. "Everything you've described can be attributed to the fact she's a three-quarter-ton. In anticipation of heavier loads, she's geared lower to handle it. The V8 is a lot of engine, but the transmission is the other half of what makes for a solid-performing truck when it comes to hauling loads."

"I suspect that's also the reason the ride was kind of hard?"

"Yep, that's also part of the package when it comes to a three-quarter-ton. With a load she'll ride almost like a car. When she's empty she's more like a tank."

Charles chuckled. *Maybe I judged you a bit harshly based on my first impression. The fact is, I like that you seem to be honest.*

"Anything else you're uncomfortable with?" Cal asked.

"The heater fan is a bit noisy. Sounds like a bearing going out, which bothers me for a truck that's only three or four years old. Other than that, I guess my biggest concern is the price. What are you willing to do there?"

Cal removed his glasses and rubbed his eyes. "That's a good question, Charles, but before we go down that road I think we should decide whether or not this is even the right truck for you."

"What have you got in mind?"

"Well, to be frank, I'm not sure you should be considering a three-quarter-ton. With your concerns about the gearing and the ride, I'm wondering if you wouldn't be a lot happier with a half-ton."

Charles shrugged. "I don't know. I'm not sure how often I'll push the capacity of a half-ton, but I'd rather have the extra capacity and not need it, rather than needing it and not having it. Besides, isn't the three-quarter-ton built to a stronger standard?"

"Most of the difference is in the suspension. There are other considerations as well, but for infrequent heavy loading I don't think the lighter components will be any problem at all."

"What are you driving at?"

"Well, Charles, I happen to have an alternative that I think you really ought to take a look at before you make a decision."

"And what would that be?"

"It's a new truck that was ordered in for another construction company. The buyer had a heart attack that has laid him up for the past few months and the truck has been sitting waiting for him to get better. At the moment I'm not sure he's ever going to be able to get back to work fulltime. That being the case, the truck is back on the market, at least for all intents and purposes."

"Man, that's tough."

"It is. But under the circumstances he'll be better off concentrating on regaining his health rather than worrying about whether or not he'll ever be able to take delivery of his special-order truck."

"Special order?"

Cal nodded. "Special order. It has all the hauling benefits of a three-quarter-ton without the downside issues with the ride."

"How exactly do you pull off that particular miracle?"

"How about I show you? It's just a short walk across the lot."

Cal led the way and Charles fell in behind. *Interesting, for the first time since I met him, he isn't shuffling.*

Cal stopped in front of a gleaming orange and white pickup. It was clearly new and Charles firmly stepped on the first niggling guilt at the thought of even considering a new pickup.

"Here she is Charles. In every way that matters she's the equivalent of the green and white three-quarter-ton. She has the same V8 engine, the same frame, even the same bed length. She also has a rather unique option that increases her carrying capacity by a thousand pounds. In case your math is a little rusty, if you add half a ton to half a ton, that gives you a full two thousand pounds of carrying capacity."

Cal gestured for Charles to follow as he knelt down in front of the rear wheel. He pointed at a set of half-size leaf springs. "These little babies are in addition to the standard coil springs on the half-ton. When you load her up, they come into play and pick up the extra load. It's brilliant really. You get the car-like ride of a half-ton with the carrying capacity and stability of a three-quarter-ton, but it only comes into effect when the load demands it."

"Interesting." Charles murmured.

"It is." Cal smiled. "But that's not the only thing." He rose to his feet and beckoned Charles to follow him to the cab. He opened the door and pointed at the steering column. "The three-speed on this truck gives you the best of both worlds. First gear is a true granny gear, giving you all the torque you need to start a heavy load, or to crawl across your fields if that's what you need. On the other hand, third gear is for cruising. When you're running empty, or even with a light load, you're going to clip right along and you're going to get far better mileage than you will from the three-quarter-ton you test-drove."

"So what's the downside?"

Cal raised a finger. "Hold that thought. Before we go there, you told me you have a family. Remember the door on the '61?"

Charles nodded.

"With the wrap-around windshield it was a tight fit climbing into the cab. Even on the passenger side. With this newly designed cab your wife has all the room in the world. Instead of feeling like she's climbing into a straitjacket, she'll feel like she's climbing into her car. What's that worth to you, Charles?"

"I'm betting not as much as the difference between the price on the two trucks."

"Maybe not, but keep in mind we've already addressed both of the complaints you have with the green and white truck."

"But what about the price?"

"Before we haggle on the price, at least take it for a drive and see for yourself that I haven't oversold this truck. Not even a little bit."

"I don't know. I'm on an awfully strict budget."

"I'm sure you are, Charles, but there's something else I know about you. You told me you're building your dairy to an eighty-cow operation. That tells me you think long term and I'm betting you'd rather have something that will keep up with your long-term plans rather than a *make do* that will just wind up holding you back. Come on, Charles, you owe it to yourself to at least check it out so you can make an informed decision."

"I don't know."

"No pressure, Charles. I promise, if you don't like it, we'll go right back to the green and white, but only if you're certain you'll be happy with it."

"I guess it couldn't hurt to drive it. It's not like I'm committing to buy it."

"No, you're not. It's just a test ride to see if it addresses the concerns you have with the three-quarter-ton. Now slip behind the wheel and drive us back to the green and white so I can grab the plates and you can take this unique little truck for a spin."

"So what do you think, Charles? Is she everything I told you she'd be?"

Charles shrugged. "I have to admit it rides a lot better than the three-quarter-ton did."

"And how do you like the way it responds to in-town driving? No pushing the engine to keep up with the flow of traffic."

"True, but there's not much range in first gear."

"I'll grant you that, but there wasn't much range in the first gear on the three-quarter-ton either." Cal winked and Charles chuckled at being caught in his feeble protest.

"OK, I admit I like this truck better than the used one, but that doesn't change what I can afford to spend on a truck. I know what the sticker on the window says, but what's the bottom line on this one?"

"Tell me this, Charles. Is the price the only thing that's keeping you from driving this truck home today?"

"It's a big part of the problem, but no, it's not the only thing."

"What else is standing in the way, Charles?"

"For one thing, I've already got a truck I have to drive home. As good as I am, I haven't figured out a way to drive two rigs at the same time."

Cal laughed. "Anything else?"

"Even if we can come together on the price, I don't have the cash right now to buy either truck. I'm going to have to sell some more stock to raise the cash I need."

"How long will that take?"

"Probably a couple of weeks."

"Hmm, that could be a problem. All our sales are on a first-come, first-served basis. Unless you're willing to finance or put down a substantial deposit, there's simply no way I can guarantee availability on either truck."

"Such is life. If either or both of them sell there are plenty of other trucks out there."

"I'm sure that's true, at least for the used truck. They won't be in the same condition and won't have the same mileage, but if you look long enough you'll probably find something comparable. This truck, on the other hand ..." Cal shrugged. "It's unusual enough that you'll have to special-order it if you want the same capabilities. I'd hate to see you miss out on it if it's the one you want."

"You've made your point, Cal, now let's cut to the chase. What's your bottom line on a cash deal?"

Cal rubbed his jaw. "You're going to think I've been stringing you along, but I promise you that I haven't been. Our sales manager is trying a new strategy of posting the lowest price in the window and that's what you get. He calls it his 'no dicker' sale."

Charles snorted. "You're kidding me, right?"

"I wish I were, Charles, but I'm not. While I'm confident our pricing is comparable to whatever you're going to be able to get other dealers to come down to for a comparably equipped truck, I promised you I'd work you a special price. In order to do that I have just one more question for you. Are you a sporting man, Charles?"

"That depends on what exactly you mean by a sporting man."

"It's no real mystery. I've spent the past few hours working with you to find the best fit for your vehicle needs. I'm willing to put every dime of my commission up on a wager. If I win, you buy this truck at the price listed in the window. If you win, I'll give you my personal check for the amount of my commission. On this truck that amounts to two hundred and sixty dollars."

"Why would you do that?"

"Because I told you I'd work with you on the price and this is the only way I can do that."

"And what exactly is this wager you want to make?"

"Just a simple race. I want to prove once and for all that this is the perfect truck for you. You can choose any truck on the lot—new, used, V6 or V8. You'll drive your choice and I'll drive this truck. We'll race a quarter mile from a standing start. If you beat me you get a substantial discount on your purchase of whatever truck you choose. If I beat you, you agree to buy the truck that I just proved will do everything you want and do it with style."

"What's the catch?"

"No catch, Charles. I'll even give you the best two out of three races."

"Stock truck? No changes or special modifications?"

Cal shook his head. "I've already told you this truck is anything but stock. That's the essence of what I'm trying to prove to you. That being said, I assure you it's a stock engine and a stock transmission. There are at least two brand-new three-quarter-ton trucks on the lot that have the same 283 V8 that this truck has. There are also an assortment of trucks with V6 engines and three-speed and four-speed transmissions. You choose, we race, and the best truck and driver wins."

"Do you pull this kind of stunt with every sale?"

"No, I don't."

"What happens if your boss finds out?"

"I'd probably get fired."

"Then why do it?"

"Because I really want to see you in this truck, and at the moment I don't see any other way to get you there."

"Well, I hate to break it to you, Cal, but I don't think this harebrained plan is going to do it either. Even if I were willing to go along with your idea, which I'm not sure I am, it will be a week or two before I can scrape the money together for even the used truck."

"We could race today and that way you'd know exactly how much you have to pull together."

"No, we can't. The fact is, I'm already going to be pushing it to make it home by chore time as it is. I'm not going to risk being late, even if I manage to smoke you and win the two-hundred-and-sixty-dollar discount."

Cal chuckled. "At least you're still thinking positive. I like that. I'll tell you what. I'll keep the offer open for two weeks or until this truck is snapped up by someone else, whichever comes first. That clears my conscience as far as having worked with you on the price. If you wait longer than two weeks, or if this truck sells before you come back, the deal's off the table. Agreed?"

Charles looked at Cal's outstretched hand. *It's one of the craziest propositions I've ever received, and I'll have to give it some serious thought before I consent, but I'm not sure there's much downside. He may be able to beat me on the first race, while I'm not completely familiar with whatever truck I choose, but he won't beat me on the second or third heat. I've been driving for years, and I'm younger and have better reflexes.* "I'll think about it."

Cal shook his head. "I have to know we have a deal. Otherwise there's no point holding the option open for the next two weeks."

"What's to keep me from agreeing to your terms and then just not bothering to show up?"

"Only one thing, Charles. I think you're an honest man, just like me."

Chapter 3

At first it had felt dishonest not to disclose everything to Emily. Charles had willingly talked to her about the three-quarter-ton he'd test-driven, but somehow he'd not been totally comfortable telling her he was considering a drag race that would ultimately dictate not only which truck he purchased but the price he paid as well. It was a childish plan, and in his most candid moments he was able to admit that was the real reason for his reluctance. The problem was, he was only able to admit it in the security of his own thoughts.

His work on the corral progressed, and the days until the next cattle sale slipped past in a blur of work that commenced before sunup and persisted until after dark. The check for the payment on the first five steers arrived on Monday, bringing with it a twinge of conscience. He ignored the unsettled feelings and they subsided under the onslaught of relentless physical work.

Charles managed to maintain his tenuous control until Wednesday morning, when Emily was once again truck-side, operating the heavy sliding door used to lock the cattle in the back of the truck. *As much as I might try to convince myself that it's my decision what pickup I buy for farm use, the fact of the matter is, Emily is just as much a part of running this farm as I am. That's the reason it's called a family farm.*

He snapped the whip, lashing a reluctant steer on its backside and urging it forward into the confines of the loading chute. It was digging with all four feet as it pushed against the cattle that had entered the chute before it. They were wedged tightly in the chute just outside the doorway into the truck. In the excitement of the loading, one of the previous yearlings had left a fresh pile of manure at the bottom of the ramp and the trailing steer kicked a fresh glob into the air, landing pocket-high across the left side of Charles' jeans. "Oh, for Pete's sake! I already smell like cow manure without having you slather it all over me."

He flicked the whip and the sharp rifle-like pop brought the lead steer's head up. In quick succession he laid the whip on the last two steers in the chute and together they were able to break the logjam and push the balky steer in the front through the open door. It was like uncorking a bottle and the other four steers pushed through right on the heels of the leader.

"Shut the door, Emily!"

The rope whistled through the pulleys and the door crashed down in the face of one of the steers that had managed to get itself turned back around and facing the open doorway.

"Good job, my dear. I'd hate to have had to face him down with nothing more than a light whip. He'd have come right over me if he'd gotten through the door."

"I'm glad we got him stopped." Emily's laughter carried easily to Charles. "I'd hate to think what kind of mess cow prints would have left up the front of your pants and shirt. It's hard enough getting your clothes clean without having the cows grind the manure in."

"Steers, dear," Charles growled. "Not cows."

"Lighten up, Charles. I know they're steers, but that doesn't change the fact that I'm glad they didn't run over you as they escaped from the truck."

"I know, because washing my clothes is already bad enough." There was a sulky edge to his voice, but Charles couldn't help it. He leaned through the fence and retrieved a stick from the ground. He used it to scrape the worst of the manure from his pants, deftly flicking it into the corral before dropping the stick back outside the fence.

"You know I'm not just worried about your clothes."

"Right. That's why you enjoy making fun of me so much."

"I might tease you, Charles, but I'd never make fun of you."

"From where I stand I don't feel much difference."

The sharpness of his retort was not lost on Emily. "I'm sorry, Charles, I didn't mean to hurt you." Her cheeks had picked up pink highlights and she was biting her lower lip. "If that's everything for the moment, I'll grab Jason and meet you on the porch with some clean pants. I'm sure you'll want to change before you head to the auction."

Charles nodded as he climbed through the pole fence.

Emily turned on her heel and disappeared around the front of the truck.

Good job, Charles. You were already feeling guilty about not telling her what you were up to. Now you've let your anger at yourself bleed over and you've snapped at your wife. It takes a real man to chew a woman out when she's doing nothing but helping you in the first place. He heaved a frustrated sigh. *It was bad enough before I shot my mouth off. Now how am I ever going to tell her what kind of mess I've gotten myself into?*

Charles dropped the yearling steers off at the auction yard, accepted the delivery receipt, and immediately left for Modern Motor. *I ought to be ringside watching to see how my cattle sell, but all I can think about is my stupid bet*

with Cal. If I don't go get the race over with now, it'll probably be too late again by the time the cattle sell. Besides, this way I can beat him, he can tell me what my discount will be, and I can be back in time to check at the office to see how they sold before I have to head home to do the chores. At least I'll have it behind me and I can quit hiding it from Emily. She'll never need to know how I got the additional discount.

Charles maneuvered the cattle truck into the Modern Motor lot and pulled to a stop near the used pickups. A quick search confirmed that the green and white '61 Chevy was sitting exactly where Charles had parked it a week ago. *So far so good. At least it looks like Cal overstated the interest in used three-quarter-ton pickups.*

As he ambled across the lot, Charles searched the rows of new pickups for any sign of the orange and white pickup Cal was so determined to sell him. He made a complete circuit of the new pickups without finding any sign of the truck. Tipping his hat back, he scratched his head. *Maybe Cal overstated the demand for used trucks, but it looks like the new one is gone.* He tugged his cap back in place as a young man emerged from the showroom door and began walking in his direction.

As he approached, he raised his hand in greeting. "I'm Andy. Is there anything I can do for you today?"

"I'm not sure," Charles replied, pushing his cap back and scratching his head. "I was in a week ago, and Cal showed me a couple of pickups. Is he around today?"

Andy glanced around the lot. "He was here earlier, but I don't see him at the moment. If you'd like to come inside I'd be happy to have him paged."

"Thanks, I'd appreciate that."

"If you don't mind my asking, what has Cal shown you?"

Charles shrugged. "I don't mind. I'm looking for a pickup and he showed me the green and white '61 you had in the paper last week. He also showed me a new orange and white pickup. That's what I was doing when you came out, checking to see what was still available since I was in last."

Andy nodded. "The green and white '61 is still here, but I'm not sure about the orange and white. Seems like it has been on at least one test drive every day for the past week or so. Lots of interest in that one."

"I noticed it's not on the lot. Has it been sold?"

"I'm not sure, but let me find Cal and he can check into it for you." Andy waved at a grouping of chairs nestled against the wall. "If you'd like to take a seat I'll page Cal."

Andy had scarcely disappeared when the door opened and Cal walked into the showroom. He looked around and, seeing Charles, made a beeline toward him, a smile blossoming on his face. Charles rose as Cal extended his hand.

"It's good to see you, Charles. How are you today?"

"I'm fine. I dropped off another load of steers at the auction and decided to stop in to see if your special pricing offer is still good. I didn't see the orange and white pickup on the lot when I drove in."

Cal smiled, his hands moving in a calming gesture. "Not to worry, Charles. It's been out on a number of test drives over the past few days and I just took it over to put some gas in it. No one has signed on the bottom line so our agreement is still on the table. Are you ready for your test drive?"

Charles shrugged. "I guess I'm as ready as I'm ever going to be."

"You seem reluctant. Having second thoughts about our agreement?"

"More like fiftieth or sixtieth thoughts. Your proposition is pretty strange. For the past week I've felt like I'm back in high school again."

Cal chuckled. "I'm sorry for making you uncomfortable."

At that moment there was a click, followed by a female voice. "Calvin Ellis to the showroom, Calvin Ellis to the showroom, please." The announcement carried to every corner of the building and echoed back from the external speakers mounted to cover the lot.

"Umm, it seems the powers that be wish to see me."

Charles smiled. "I suspect that's just to tell you that I'm here."

Cal nodded, understanding dawning in his eyes. "You're probably right, but if I don't show up for the message, Mabel is going to keep right on making the announcement and a lot of people are going to get needlessly annoyed. If you'll excuse me for a moment, I'll be right back."

Charles nodded and resumed his seat. His eyes were drawn to the cherry-red Chevelle parked on his side of the showroom. *At the moment I'd a lot rather be making a deal on a new car for Emily than a pickup for me. I've been testy and short-tempered all week. I don't dare tell her what I've been up to, and that's probably what's got me so on edge. A new car would be a nice way to tell her I'm sorry for being such a jerk.*

Cal walked into view, pulling Charles from his introspection.

"You were right. The page was to tell me you are here." Cal handed Charles a pen and a printed sheet of paper. "This is a test-drive release. I need you to fill in your address and phone number and sign and date the bottom. I'll fill in the VIN and description when you decide which pickup you want to take for your solo test drive."

Charles nodded and started filling out the form.

"Before you decide, I thought I'd mention we got a new delivery this past week. There was a blue 1/2 ton short-bed sport truck that came in on the shipment. It's got a 283 V8 with a four-speed transmission. It's the only other half-ton on the lot with a V8. I don't want you thinking I'm taking advantage in any way by pushing you to a heavier, lower-geared three-quarter-ton."

"It's good of you to mention it. It sounds like just
what I'm looking for. Let's go take a look, and if it's what
you describe I think I'd like to test-drive it."

"Very good. If you'll come with me I'll show it to
you."

Charles followed Cal north on the Yellowstone
Highway. Passing beyond the city limits, they took a road
heading east towards the mountains that lined the
southeastern edge of the Snake River Plain. He was in the
blue short-bed and was finding it every bit as responsive
as he had hoped it would be. The transmission shifted
smoothly and the V8 provided plenty of power. *I almost
feel sorry for Cal, taking his commission away from him this
way, but he's a grown man and knew what he was letting
himself in for when he proposed the race in the first place.*

Cal turned south and drove for about half a mile. He
pulled off to the shoulder of the road where it passed
through a sagebrush-covered sand dune. He climbed out
of the orange and white truck and motioned for Charles
to pull in behind him. Cal leaned against the bed of the
pickup, waiting for Charles to join him.

"This is about as secluded a section of road as we'll
find anywhere near town." He pointed back to the north.
"See that rise in the road? Just beyond the crest is a
power pole and off to the west is a fence line. They're
about twenty to thirty feet apart, and the fence line is
pretty close to a quarter mile."

Charles nodded. "So we race from here to the fence
line?"

"That would be my recommendation. There's a house
a little further up the road so there's some risk of them
calling the cops, but if you look off to the south the road
turns into gravel right there. I'd rather we have plenty of
room to slow down without having to worry about
running out of pavement."

"Makes sense to me. Besides, if we don't lollygag too much, we should be well out of here before any cops can show up."

Cal nodded. "Once we start, we run the heats one right after the other. We'll calculate the winner as the first one to pass the fence line. We'll slow down and turn around on the main road. Come back here and we'll turn around and run the next heat."

"Sounds good."

"One more thing, Charles. I don't want you to think I'm taking advantage so I'll let you call the start of the race."

Charles' eyebrows shot up in surprise. "That's decent of you, Cal, but maybe it would be more fair if we take turns."

"Suit yourself, but I'm willing to let you start each race."

"I'm fine with taking turns."

"In that case, you take the first and third heat. I'll take the second one. I'll take the wrong side of the road and I'll roll down my passenger window to make it easier for me to hear. Just be sure to call it loudly enough for these old ears."

"How about I drop my hand at the same time so you've got a visual cue?"

Cal shook his head. "I want both of your hands available for driving and I don't want either of us looking to the side when the race starts. Keep your eyes on the road so we don't accidentally mess up either one of these brand-new trucks. That would cost me my job for certain."

"We don't want that. I'll make sure you can hear me."

"Good enough. Let's get this show on the road."

They jockeyed the two trucks into position, side by side pointing north on the narrow road.

Charles rolled his window down and shouted across the gap. "Can you hear me all right?"

Cal nodded and signaled to go ahead.

"One."

Cal revved the engine on his truck.

"Two," Charles shouted, and once again the engine of the orange and white truck roared.

"Three," Charles yelled, uncertain if Cal could hear him.

"Go!" He mashed the accelerator pedal and released the clutch. The tires squealed as they sought purchase against the asphalt. The tires grabbed and as the pitch of the engine rose, Charles speed-shifted into second gear. He was the first off the mark and the front end of the orange and white pickup faded from his peripheral vision. With no tachometer, Charles was focused on the sound of the engine to let him know when to shift into third gear.

His eyes were glued to the road ahead and he was just about to grab third gear when he caught the movement in the corner of his eye. The orange and white pickup was moving up and starting to pass him. Charles shifted into third and for a split second he was coasting on his momentum and the other pickup increased its lead, nosing ahead and continuing to accelerate.

Charles buried the accelerator and the truck started to fishtail as the tires broke free for a few precious heartbeats until he could back off the accelerator and ramp it up more smoothly. It couldn't have been more than two or three seconds but that was all it took. Charles pushed the truck hard, catching fourth gear just before the fence line flashed past on his left, but he was at least two vehicle lengths behind the already decelerating orange and white pickup.

"Smooth move, Charles. If you hadn't lost your head and panicked you'd have taken him. It would have been close, but having to back off right in the middle of the race cost you the win."

Charles arrived at the stop sign well ahead of Cal. The adrenaline had kicked in and his hands were starting to shake as he turned the truck around and headed back to the cut that marked the starting line. He was in position at the starting line when Cal pulled up next to him and stopped.

Cal leaned out his window, nearly crossing the small gap between the trucks. "That was a good try, Charles. It looked like you had me there for a moment. If you wouldn't object to a little friendly advice, you're trying too hard. You broke loose at the start and again partway down the course. Spinning your tires doesn't move you ahead as fast as keeping your grip on the road will."

Charles nodded, his bruised pride smarting as Cal made a three-point turn and jockeyed the orange and white pickup into position at the starting line.

"Can you hear me OK?" Cal called across his cab and the space separating the trucks.

"Yes," Charles yelled in response.

"One," Cal called loudly, romping on the engine and letting it settle back to near idle.

"Two." The cadence was slower than when Charles had called the countdown, but Cal was clearly matching the count to the revving of his engine.

Two can play this game. Charles prepared to rev his engine in synchronization with Cal's pickup.

"Three." The count came as the engine was ramping up. The engine noise subsided and started to build again.

"Go!" The call was more imagined than heard but Charles didn't hesitate. He released the clutch and carefully matched the acceleration to the grip of the tires. There wasn't any of the hopping and bouncing that had accompanied the first start, and once again the competing pickup dropped from view and he accelerated down the ribbon of road that stretched a half mile ahead of him.

He had caught third gear and was still powering ahead when the nose of the orange and white truck appeared beside his shoulder. *How can this be? I was even further ahead than last time and he still caught up with me!* Charles kept pressing the accelerator, pushing the ragged edge of the truck's traction, but it was no use. The orange and white truck walked past him, its engine roaring and building toward the crescendo marking the shift to the next gear.

Charles was already at the point of pushing the engine beyond its designed operating RPM and he speed-shifted into fourth gear. Even the big V8 lacked sufficient torque to spin the tires in fourth gear, so mashing the accelerator to the floor did nothing more than push his acceleration curve as quickly as the engine RPMs could rebuild. He was a little over a truck length behind and he could feel the momentum of the race shifting as the fence line flashed by.

The orange and white truck dipped as Cal cut his acceleration and fell in behind the blue sport truck as Charles pulled easily past him. *I can't believe it. I didn't do anything wrong that time and he still beat me. The engines are evenly matched and my vehicle actually weighs less. I should have taken him that time.* Charles swallowed. *But I didn't.* The realization that stole over him was a cold, sick thing in the pit of his stomach. *Cal said the best two out of three races. I just lost two in a row. There's no point even running the third heat. I just committed to buy a brand-new pickup that I can't afford.*

Charles pulled up to the stop sign and looked in the rearview mirror. Cal's arm was stuck out his window and he was signaling for Charles to turn around for the third heat. Charles shook his head. *There's no point heaping any more humiliation on myself. We just as well head back to the dealership and sign the papers.* Charles turned on the left turn signal and was just starting to make the turn when he saw Cal open the door of his truck and start jogging toward him.

Charles mashed the clutch to the floor and braked the truck to a stop.

Cal was out of breath when he arrived and held up a finger as he sucked in a couple of deep breaths. "That was a good heat, Charles. Considering the fact that you went through all four gears, I think you actually out-drove me."

Charles shook his head. "That's not what the finish line said. Besides, you've already beaten me twice in a row. There's no point running a third heat. Let's head back to Modern Motor and I'll purchase your truck."

"Listen, Charles, this was supposed to be a friendly competition. By your tone it hasn't worked out quite that way and I don't want to sell the truck with you feeling this way. I'll tell you what. We'll throw out the first race as you weren't familiar with your ride. I think the fact that it's a short bed made it lighter than you expected. We'll race one more time. Winner take all."

"No, we had a deal. I'm man enough to take my medicine when I make a mistake."

"Come on, Charles. Don't go all surly on me. I want you to want this truck. I want you to come back and buy that red Chevelle you were drooling over in the showroom. I want you to think of me as a friend you want your other friends to buy their cars from."

"Look, Cal, I appreciate what you're saying and trying to do, but the fact is, I ran the best race I could in the second heat. There isn't any way to coax any more speed out of this truck. I don't know how you did it, but I'm clearly outmatched."

"If I share my secret, are you willing to give it one more try?"

Charles stomped on his retort, feeling like he was already crawling across broken glass without the additional humiliation of being told what he was doing wrong. "I don't see the point, Cal." His voice was sharp and impatient, even to his own ears, but Cal seemed not to hear it.

"You are starting out in first gear. I'm not. With a V8, these trucks have plenty of power to start off in second gear. It's not the rabbit start you're getting off to, but it's one less gear you have to go through getting to the top end."

Charles shook his head like he had been punched. *Of course! Why didn't I think of that? Once he gets rolling he rides the power band with fewer interruptions for shifting. If I had gotten to fourth quicker I'd have taken him.*

Cal smiled. "You've figured it out, haven't you? So how about that third heat before the cops get here?"

Charles nodded grimly. "You're on."

Charles maneuvered the sport truck into position and waited impatiently while Cal got the orange and white truck pulled up next to him.

"You ready?" Cal hollered.

"As ready as I'll ever be. Let's do this!"

Charles shifted into second gear and started his count.

"One." He revved the engine, letting it fall back to idle as he waited, matching his cadence to what Cal had done at the start of the second heat.

"Two." He revved the engine again, his heart throbbing in harmony with the rumbling engine. *I have every advantage this time. I'm calling the start. I have the lighter vehicle and faster reflexes. With both of us starting in second gear I'm finally going to take him. It seems a bit unsportsmanlike, but at this point I'll take the win any way I can get it.*

"Three." The sound of the two engines revving in unison was almost deafening. They came off the power band and Charles pressed the accelerator again.

The roar of the engines was building as he screamed, "Go!" He mashed the accelerator to the floor as he released the clutch. The sound of the engine changed subtly as it took the drag of the transmission and started to drive the truck forward.

It wasn't a rabbit start by any stretch of the imagination, but he was still first off the line. *Second in this truck must be geared a little lower than it is in the orange and white truck. He may have just cost himself the race!* Charles rode the power band of the engine and speed-shifted into third as the engine began to howl at its mistreatment. In the heartbeats it took for the engine to accept the greater load, the orange and white truck crept into his peripheral vision.

Charles kept his foot on the accelerator, coaxing every RPM he could out of the engine. Slowly, almost inexorably, the orange and white pickup inched forward. Drawing abreast of him, it started to pull away. *It all comes down to this. One final shift. If I wait too long I'll never get back on the power band in time to pull ahead. If I go too soon, he'll have enough of a lead that I'll never catch him.*

Charles listened to the pitch of the engine as it rose from its throaty roar to a shrieking howl. He mashed the clutch to the floor and jerked back on the shifting lever. The transmission shifted and he popped the clutch, the accelerator still glued to the floor. The orange and white truck was half a length ahead, but the sport truck was finding itself. The momentum shifted and the orange and white truck stopped inching ahead. Slowly, one roaring second after another the blue truck began to overtake its nemesis. Charles' hands were clamped to the steering wheel with white-knuckle intensity. The front bumper was just pulling alongside the cab of the orange and white pickup when it dipped and began decelerating.

Charles' big-picture vision snapped back in place as the fence line marking the end of the race receded in his rearview mirror. "I'll be damned. He beat me again!" Charles backed off the accelerator and allowed the truck to coast toward the stop sign. He was peripherally aware as the orange and white pickup pulled in behind him and followed along as Charles pulled to a stop at the edge of the intersection.

Cal was out of his truck and approaching the blue pickup before Charles had a chance to consider whether or not he should proceed on to the dealership. Cal reached through the open window and slapped Charles on the shoulder.

"That was incredible. I would have never believed you could coax that kind of performance out of a four-speed. If you'd have had ten more seconds you would have taken me."

Charles shook his head, mentally trying to catch up with the verbal barrage. "What are you talking about? I drove a perfect race and you still smoked me."

"Yeah, but the point is it wasn't by nearly as much as it should have been. That orange and white truck is as close to a perfect quarter-mile racer as has ever been built. The V8 is plenty big enough to get it off the line in second gear and the engine and transmission are perfectly matched to ride the power band all the way to the end of the quarter mile. Don't you get it, Charles? I haven't been shifting. I start in second and finish in second. I don't have the reflexes any more to be able to shift, even if I wanted to. I didn't beat you through skill, I beat you because the truck is that much better suited to this kind of race than any other truck on our lot. Heck, for that matter there's probably not many cars that could take it in a quarter mile."

"So this was all a setup?"

Cal shrugged. "Pretty much, I guess. I never really expected you to make a race of it, and for that matter I never really intended to hold you to our bet. My hope was that you or some other young buck would see the potential of this particular truck and would snap it up to take advantage of their friends. I figured as a farmer you were a long shot, but you were young enough that I figured it was worth a shot anyway."

"Wait a minute. You've pulled this ploy on other suckers as well."

"Suckers? No. I extended the wager to a couple of others but you were the only one so far who has taken me up on it."

"I'll be—"

"Not if you don't say it." Cal chuckled. He glanced around, concern plain on his face. "But we really do need to get out of here. After three heats I'm sure we've worn out our welcome. Screaming up and down this narrow road at sixty miles an hour is certain to raise the hackles of any nearby adults. I'd hate to have to explain how a man of my advanced maturity was involved in such juvenile activity."

Charles snorted. "You're a real piece of work. What do you expect us to do now? Sneak back to Modern Motor and have a shouting match about whether or not I buy your truck?"

"Not exactly, Charles. I'd still like to sell you a truck, but not one that you insist on referring to as 'mine.' As long as you are thinking of it in those terms, you'll never be happy with it."

"And what about our bet?"

"I've already told you I won't hold you to it. It wasn't the fairest wager after all."

"Maybe not, but I'm a big boy. I knew the risks when I shook your hand to seal the bargain."

"Be that as it may, we really need to get out of here. We're close enough to town that it won't take all that long for the county to get a deputy out here. I for one don't want to get caught driving a truck that matches the description of one driven by a couple of hormone-crazed teenagers."

Charles chuckled. "I'll meet you back at the lot. One way or the other I'll buy a truck. You've earned at least that much."

Epilogue

October 17, 1975

The waning moon hung suspended less than a handbreadth above the western horizon. From the vantage point of the foothills on its eastern flank, the great Snake River Plain stretched out to the west and north as far as the horizon and beyond. With the yellow third-quarter moon so low in the sky, the stars should have been far brighter and more numerous than were presently visible. Looking to the north, the stars glittered brightly like diamond chips against the black vault of the sky. To the south, evident by the way they erased the stars from the sky, a massive wall of black clouds marched rapidly towards the northeast. It was going to be a race as to whether the moon would be extinguished by its setting or blotted from the sky by the oncoming storm clouds.

On the hillside below the autumn sky, all was strangely quiet. Barely a whisper of breeze preceded the buffeting winds racing ahead of the storm front. The lights of the cities, towns, villages, and farms stretched out for scores of miles across the valley floor. Car lights crawled along the roads and highways that crisscrossed the area like a giant's checkerboard.

The harvest of the dry farm wheat had been completed weeks earlier, and the fields were reduced to vast swaths of stubble that wound around and over the contours of the foothills that reared up into the Rocky Mountains. Not far from the mouth of Wolverine Canyon, in a stubble field that backed up against a stand of quaking aspen, sat a pickup truck.

It was a 1964 Chevrolet C-10 Fleetside, painted in orange and white and trimmed in chrome. The lights were out, and the engine was off, making the vehicle hard to pick out of the darkening night. The only light was the faint glow given off by the AM radio which provided a steady stream of rock 'n' roll Top 40 hits.

Fifteen-year-old Jason Tucker lay sprawled behind the wheel, eyes closed, fast asleep. The current song wound down, and the disc jockey's resonant baritone filled the cab. "It's the top of the hour, and the hits keep coming at you, right here on your 50,000 watt super station, KOMA, 1520 kilocycles on your AM dial. This is Johnny Dark, and my gig is up for the night, so I'll be signing off until tomorrow evening at six o'clock, but don't fret, after our break for the news, Buddy Scott will be taking over, spinning your favorite hits until the sun comes up! Until tomorrow, keep it between the white lines, and keep your dial tuned to 1520, where we bring you all the hits ... all the time!"

The network identification tones sounded, and as the practiced voice of the network news anchor began reciting the lead story, a great multi-forked flash of lightning arced across the southern sky. The brilliance of the lightning lit up the night as if it were noontime, and a half-dozen heartbeats later, the booming rumble of thunder shook the ground and rocked the pickup.

Jason's eyes flew open in uncomprehending alarm as his sleep-addled brain tried to make some sense of his unfamiliar surroundings. His eyes flitted about the dimly lit cab as the dregs of sleep were banished by the surge of adrenaline coursing through his veins in response to the ground-shaking thunder that was only now beginning to subside.

His thoughts were skittering around in his head like a pat of butter tossed into a too-hot frying pan. They seemed to jump and dance as if with a mind of their own. It felt as though he were a spectator rather than the director of his own thoughts. It was not a feeling he particularly cared to experience, but for some reason he seemed powerless to wrest control over his thoughts. Maybe it was as simple as the abruptness of his awakening after his unintended slumber.

Jason had come to this secluded spot to be alone and to think. There were all too few opportunities to pause and just think about his life and to try to figure out what might lie ahead in his future. With all the work inherent in a dairy farm, and the way his dad was always on his case, Jason had precious little time to do anything other than work, attend school, and get a few hours of sleep at night. Tonight was supposed to be an exception, and it was pretty clear how well that had worked out!

Jason's thoughts took him back to earlier this evening, and his attendance at the Harvest Ball. He'd been looking forward to the dance for weeks. Granted, his feelings had been decidedly mixed as he had fantasized about an evening with Cassidy Sullivan. On one hand, he had been almost giddy at the thought of dancing with his arms around the girl of his dreams. On the other hand, he had shrunk in cold, shaking terror at the thought of actually asking her to the dance. Cassidy had to be the prettiest girl in school, at least in Jason's opinion, and he was fairly certain his opinion was at no risk of dying of loneliness.

The past several weeks he had planned and schemed and tried to figure out the best way to ask Cassidy to the dance. Try as he might, Jason had been unable to divine the proper method or find the necessary courage to move beyond the planning stage. The inevitable result was that Jason had found himself stuck in an unachievable fantasy. In fact, it was a fantasy that would never be realized, as Jason had discovered all too clearly on the day he found out one of the football jocks had already asked Cassidy to the Harvest Ball.

Hot anger stirred somewhere south of his belly at the renewed realization that he had missed his chance to spend an evening with Cassidy. The anger burned anew as he considered the audacity of a jock attending the Harvest Ball. By long tradition, the Harvest Ball was the annual opportunity for the less popular kids to step above their lowly station, even if only temporarily, and dare to spend an evening with someone in the loftier social circles. Jason was forced to admit, albeit ever so reluctantly, that Cassidy was so far beyond his own social status that there had never been any real chance she would say yes to his invitation. Yet, in spite of the painfully obvious facts, Jason had allowed himself to dream, and to hold out hope, no matter how thin that hope might have been.

Jason squirmed in the seat, and an audible sigh escaped as he mentally castigated himself. *It serves me right. The son of a dairy farmer has no right to think of dating a girl as beautiful and cultured as Cassidy, especially when she is out of my league. What could I have possibly been thinking?* Jason shook his head morosely. *The truth is, I wasn't thinking. At least not with my head.* Jason knew he had been leading with his heart, and that was a stupid thing to do. It left him vulnerable in a way no teenager ever wanted to be vulnerable, and the resulting hurt had cut deeply. In fact, the hurt still consumed him whenever he allowed his mind to wander into the well-worn grooves his thoughts had so frequently traversed over the past couple weeks.

He had dreaded the thought of attending the dance, but for good or bad, Jason had worked up the courage to tell his dad he wanted to borrow the pickup to take a date to the dance. As he had expected, Dad had turned him every which way but loose. He had to know every detail.

Who was the girl? How long had he known her? Where did she live? What were his plans for dinner? Did he plan to give her a corsage? When would he be picking her up? It seemed the questions had been endless, and Jason had been able to provide far too few satisfactory answers to his father's grilling. Yet somehow, Jason had a funny feeling that his dad hadn't been as opposed to the idea of a date as his endless questioning clearly indicated. Jason gave a soft snort at the thought. *Next to girls, parents have to be the hardest people in the world to understand!*

The evening would have been dismal enough having to go stag to the dance but at least he had hoped to enjoy some music, eat some refreshments, and maybe even have a dance or two as his consolation prize for failing to secure a date with Cassidy. Alas, it was not to be. All of his cheerful self-delusion had gone up in a puff of smoke the moment Cassidy had glided in on the arm of her date. The room had closed in on him until finally Jason had no choice but to flee to some private hideaway where he could lick his wounds and tend to his badly bruised pride. No girl should be worth this kind of humiliation and heartbreak but try as he might, Jason simply couldn't get past the fact that Cassidy was worth any price, no matter how dear.

Lightning flashed among the roiling clouds, and Jason's eyes snapped wide open at the same time his pupils tried to screw themselves down into the smallest possible opening. The follow-up thunder was less severe than the thundering clap that had awoken him so abruptly, but it seemed to rumble on forever. Jason blinked his eyes in a vain attempt to erase the afterimage which was indelibly etched in his vision. The blue-white lines effectively blotted out everything inside the cab of the pickup, and Jason realized for the first time just how dark it was. When he had parked at the edge of this field, to give himself an opportunity to think, the moon had been a good three hours from setting. Now his eyes sought in vain for any hint of the moon. Alarm bells began to go off in his mind as he realized the moon had set. *Dad was very clear that I am to be home by 1:00 a.m., and not one second later. If I'm late he's going to kill me!* Jason's left hand stretched out and twisted the knob that controlled the dome light in the cab. The light came on and Jason quickly checked his watch. *Twelve fourteen.* His stomach unclenched ever so slightly. *There's still time to make it home before my curfew, even if I have to push the speed limit a bit.*

Taking a steadying breath, Jason turned the key to start the truck. The engine turned over with a sluggishness that warned of a seriously low battery. As the slow groaning of the starter penetrated his addled thoughts, Jason's right hand released the key so quickly you would have thought he was pulling back from a red-hot branding iron. *Great, just great! This can't be happening. On top of everything else, I'm going to get stuck here because I fell asleep with the radio on and ran the stupid battery down. Now I'm not only going to be late, I'm going to be really late. I won't even be able to head home until someone comes along and finds me. The way my luck is going that will be tomorrow morning at the earliest.*

Jason gripped the steering wheel so hard his knuckles began to whiten. *Father in Heaven, don't let this happen. I can't deal with this right now and I certainly can't face Dad if I am stuck here until someone comes along who can give me a jump.* Jason consciously relaxed his grip on the wheel and was amazed to find the panic that had seized him began to subside and his thoughts began to flow more rationally.

I have to stop the power drain. Action followed thought, and he killed the radio and the overhead light. Jason opened the driver side door and climbed stiffly out of the seat. *Sleeping in the cab of this stupid truck is certainly not the most comfortable place I've ever slept.* Doing his best to ignore his cramped muscles, Jason moved to the front of the pickup and opened the hood. As he did so, a gust of wind slammed into his right side and nearly jerked the hood out of his hands. *That would be the perfect ending to the perfect day! All I need is for the wind to rip the hood off the truck. I can see Dad's face as I drive in tomorrow morning, late, hood riding in the bed of the truck, oh yeah that would be perfect!* The hood settled at its full extension and Jason let go. It quivered noticeably in the rising wind, but it felt like it was going to remain attached, at least for the moment.

Jason felt around blindly for the battery. His fingers found the battery and sought out the cables attached to the posts. He grasped the first post and gave it a twist. *Solid, well it was certainly worth checking to see if it was loose.* Jason's fingers continued to search and found the second terminal. Lightning flashed and Jason's abused eyes were able to make out the small minus symbol embossed next to the battery post. Jason grasped the connector and cable in both hands and was almost shocked when the connector rotated a full quarter turn.

At 15 years old, Jason had been milking cows and hauling hay for years. Say what you want, one thing most anyone would have to admit was that Jason had formidable upper body strength. Pushing down with every ounce of his 165 pounds that he could bring to bear, Jason twisted the cable clamp back and forth in tiny arcs. He felt the clamp becoming more and more difficult to turn as it settled further onto the tapered battery post. "Now if I just had a wrench so I could tighten up the bolt." A thin smile pulled at the corners of his mouth as he mused, "Of course, if I am going to be wishing, I might as well wish the cable hadn't been loose in the first place!"

Satisfied that he had done all he could to tighten the loose battery connection, Jason closed the hood and returned to the cab. The wind was rising steadily, but closing the door blocked at least some of the howl that was rising with the wind. Offering a silent, almost unconscious plea for divine assistance, Jason turned the key. He half expected the slow and labored starter noise of his first attempt but was pleasantly surprised at the increased speed with which the engine was turning over. After cranking for five to ten seconds Jason realized the engine was not going to catch.

"What's wrong?" he wondered aloud. "Why won't it start?" His eyes swept the dashboard and paused on the choke, a flash of insight lighting his mind. "I must be even more flustered than I realized. I've started this old truck hundreds of times and I can't remember the last time I forgot to choke it when it was cold." Drawing a deep breath in through his mouth, Jason pulled the choke halfway out and tried the engine again. The engine cranked over several times, and then caught. Jason gunned the engine to make sure it was responding and then reduced the choke partway as the engine smoothed out.

That was way too close for comfort, Jason thought, as he checked the indicators on the dash. The generator was charging and the oil pressure was displaying a solid 30 pounds. Jason breathed a tiny sigh of relief. The temperature gauge was all the way to the cold side and Jason made a mental note to release the last half-inch on the choke once the engine warmed up. Jason pulled the knob to turn on the exterior lights and the headlights stabbed out into the darkness, adding their illumination to that of the ever more frequent lightning. *Now if I can get out of this field without getting stuck, or something equally stupid, I should have a pretty good chance of getting home before my curfew. Even if I am a little bit late, I should make it before Dad totally blows his cool.* Jason shook his head ruefully and the first hint of a real smile raised the corners of his mouth. *Either way, getting home tonight sure beats the heck out of not getting home until sometime tomorrow!*

Jason grasped the gear shift handle on the right side of the steering column, depressed the clutch and shifted the transmission into first gear. Easing out on the clutch, Jason pressed on the accelerator and pulled smoothly forward across the stubble.

Two weeks shy of his 16th birthday, Jason drove with the practiced assurance of a farm kid who had been driving tractors and trucks from the time he was seven or eight years old. Jason was proud of his driving ability. In fact he was almost as proud of his driving skill as he was of the driver's license sitting in his wallet. Although he could not legally drive at night until he turned 16, it was common practice for farm boys to drive whenever they were needed, regardless of whether the sun was up or down. Jason had been driving at night for over a year, and the fact that he could not legally do so was the thought that was furthest from his mind as he sought the gate leading to the road.

The first rain drops hit the windshield a few minutes before Jason found the gate. By the time he reached the gate the rain was coming down steadily. Jason jumped from the truck, opened the gate, climbed back into the truck and pulled through the gate and onto the road. Setting the park brake, Jason quickly closed the gate and climbed back into the relative comfort of the pickup. It might be on the cold side still but at least it was dry. After even the brief exposure of opening and closing the access gate, Jason was thoroughly soaked and starting to shiver as the outside temperature continued to drop.

As Jason released the park brake and started forward, he realized that the rain and the wind had both increased. The rain was moving almost horizontally and was running in a thin sheet that completely covered the road. "Not the very best conditions for making up lost time," he mused. "At least the electrical system seems to be working, and the engine has finally warmed up, so I see no reason why I can't make myself more comfortable." Jason killed the last of the choke and turned on the heater. As the fan kicked in, the welcome warmth engulfed his feet and began to make its way up his legs. *A little more of this and my shivering should stop. It seems things are actually starting to look up.*

Jason continued down out of the foothills, traveling mostly in second gear due to the twists and turns of the narrow road. Never known as a speed demon, the truck still did a respectable job in second gear. By pushing things a bit, Jason could reach 45 to 50 miles an hour in second gear. He was sure it wasn't the best way to treat the engine or transmission but it did give him reasonable control and he could use the engine to help him decelerate without having to use the brakes on what was quickly becoming a very slick road.

Thinking ahead, Jason reviewed the remainder of the journey in his mind. A few more miles and he would reach the bottom. Once on the flat, it was just a mile or so to the intersection where he would turn north. A couple of miles to the substation, another five or so to the sugar factory, a couple more miles to the Yellowstone Highway, through town, and then he could open it back up and be home in another 10 to 15 minutes.

Perhaps it was the fact his mind was wandering from his driving, perhaps it was the worsening road conditions as the temperature dropped and the rain turned into sleet, with black ice lurking only a degree or two away. Regardless, Jason was totally unprepared as he cornered and the back end of the truck started skipping sideways across the road.

Fear gripped his guts as adrenaline flooded his system and the back end of the pickup continued to come around until the vehicle was traveling almost sideways down the road. Turning frantically into the skid, Jason felt the tires begin to bite and almost in slow motion the truck began to recover. Backing off on the accelerator, Jason bled off speed as he continued his descent to the valley floor ahead. He was really shaking now, only it wasn't from the cold. It was sheer terror at how close he'd come to piling the truck into the rocks and trees that lined the narrow road.

Determined to drive more cautiously, at least until the road straightened out, Jason continued down the road out of the foothills. Visibility was anything but good as Jason approached the four-way intersection south of the substation. Looking both ways, at least as well as he could under the conditions, Jason braked at the stop sign and then headed north. The rain was continuing to fall in torrents but it seemed there was less sleet at this lower elevation. Despite his recent fear-induced caution, his need to get home by his curfew goaded him. Dropping the truck into third gear, he began to push to make up the time he had lost in the descent from the foothills. Jason was traveling better than 70 miles an hour when he passed the electrical substation. Even so, all was going well until he felt the back end of the truck start to vibrate and then it began to skip sideways across the road.

Jason felt the skid coming and let off the accelerator as he turned into the skid. Unfortunately, at 70 miles an hour on a road covered with water, there simply wasn't enough friction or time to recover. The truck began to spin, swapping ends as it went through first one, then a second, then a third complete rotation as it continued to travel north down the road. *This could be the big one!* Jason's mind screamed. It was all happening so quickly and yet it seemed as if time had slowed and Jason was sitting outside himself as a passive observer, watching events unfold in slow motion. Somewhere deep down in his soul, Jason knew that no matter how good his driving skills, there was absolutely nothing he could do to affect the outcome. He knew he should be jabbering in fear, but it was with almost clinical detachment that Jason watched events unfold.

As the truck was completing its fourth rotation, the bead on the right rear tire separated and the tire went flat almost instantly. The tire blowing should have flipped the truck and started it rolling but somehow it straightened out somewhat and settled into an uncontrolled fishtailing which had the one redeeming virtue that at least the front end of the vehicle was pointed in the same direction it was traveling. Although Jason was unaware, and certainly did not have time to check the speedometer, the speed had bled off to about 58 miles an hour when the wild ride came to an abrupt end.

The out-of-control pickup nosed off the road and the front tires sank into the rain-drenched shoulder of the road. The back end of the truck began to come around the driver's side in an end-for-end swap that was interrupted as the truck began to roll. At that moment the truck struck a power pole a couple of feet behind the cab. The impact had the effect of canceling the roll and dropping the truck back onto what remained of its shredded tires. With the engine and cab being heavier than the empty bed, the truck's momentum caused the front end to slew around the pole, which saved it from being snapped off like a toothpick. The speed had been further diminished to something around 45 miles per hour as the truck careened across the borrow pit and the front bumper struck a massive boulder on the other side. The forward speed was stopped in an instant and transferred into upward lift that raised the back end of the truck high into the air before it slowed, reversed direction, and slammed back down in a bone-jarring crash that finally silenced the tearing and rending of metal that had begun with the impact against the power pole.

The wires on the swaying power pole came together and a sheet of blue flame erupted from the electrical discharge. Its brilliance rivaled the lightning strikes that were bouncing from cloud to cloud and geysering upward from the ground to the boiling clouds. The visible electrical discharge spread from the point of contact, racing up and down the power lines paralleling the road. The blue flame traveling south reached the substation, overwhelmed the breakers in the circuit and triggered a massive overload that consumed transformers and distribution equipment as if they had been hit by a bomb. A pillar of flame billowed into the sky and rolled back on itself creating the mushroom shaped cloud formation that marks such large explosions.

The sheet of flame traveling north continued on into the distance towards the sugar factory, eventually dissipating as it struck a three-phase transformer array which was powering a large irrigation pump. The pump, along with every light and electrical appliance in an area covering several hundred square miles, was extinguished by the loss of power from the severely damaged substation.

The drumming rain mixed with the steam escaping from the punctured radiator, shredded as the rotating fan drove into the radiator when the engine mounts broke loose, slewing the engine forward in the engine compartment. The engine had ground to a halt but not before a blade broke off the fan and spun into the battery casing, opening a wound that bled the electrolytic acid solution onto the ground.

As relative silence settled over the scene, a barely conscious and badly hurt Jason tried to comprehend what had happened. His head had struck the window in the driver's door when the truck hit the power pole and had subsequently struck the windshield when the truck impacted on the boulder. The only thing that had saved Jason from instant death was the seatbelt secured across his lap. Unfortunately it lacked the restraining protection of a shoulder harness, which was not standard equipment on the aging pickup. The result was internal injuries that were far more serious than the visible cuts, bruises, and broken bones that were all too obvious. The headlights dimmed as the essential electrolyte bled out of the battery, and Jason could tell through his shock that he was failing just as rapidly as the lights were.

Out of the night, lit only by the flash of lightning and the failing headlights, a large man in a leather flight jacket strode up to the pickup. Grasping the door handle, the man opened the jammed door which should have been more than a match for even his obvious strength. The blast of cold air from the open door hammered Jason back to a semblance of lucidity and he struggled to look at his rescuer through the veil of blood flowing from his lacerated scalp. Jason attempted to shake his head to help clear his muddled brain but gave up with a groan as pain and nausea swept over him. The flight-jacketed stranger looked tenderly at the young man as the last of the battery acid drained away and the lights went dark.

Jason felt himself swimming back from some great black abyss, drawn towards someone who was insistently calling his name. Jason opened his eyes but could see little in the darkness. He could make out the form of a man standing beside him but there were no details. The man had produced a white handkerchief and was gently cleaning Jason's face as he spoke quietly. The ministrations of the handkerchief had restored some of his vision but Jason still could not see clearly. "Who are you? I can't see you."

The man paused, looked around for a moment as if to assure himself that they were alone, and reached past the open door to rest his left hand on the hood of the pickup. As he did so, the headlights flashed back on, stabbing defiantly into the darkness. The man reached over with his right hand and turned the knob which activated the dome light. In the illumination, Jason could see the man was younger than he first imagined. He looked to be in his early thirties. He was tall—Jason estimated he was six foot one—and his broad shoulders filled the open doorway from side to side. Jason was aware the rain was continuing to pour down, but somehow the rain didn't seem to be getting on the man, or on Jason for that matter. His mind tried to focus on the anomaly but somehow it just didn't seem important and he quickly lost interest.

Jason knew he was in bad shape. He was light-headed, almost dizzy, and in spite of the shock he was feeling the pain from his cuts, bruises, and broken bones. Unless he was badly mistaken, his left arm and leg were both broken and he suspected he had multiple broken ribs. In fact, there was a peculiar heaviness in his chest that was making it difficult to breathe, and all but impossible to speak.

As he labored for breath, the man reached out and laid his right hand gently on Jason's left shoulder. It was amazing! It felt like a soft warm blanket was spreading over him, starting at his shoulder, running across his body, his right arm, down his legs and feet, and up his neck to the crown of his head. Jason's breathing eased and his thinking was clearer as was his vision.

Jason studied the man more closely, he seemed hauntingly familiar. In a flash of insight Jason knew where he'd seen the man before. *He looks just like the man in the picture on mother's piano. He looks exactly like my grandpa Moyer!* Jason knew the man couldn't be Grandpa Moyer as he had died when his plane was shot down during World War II, when Jason's mother was only six years old.

Wanting desperately to know, but fearing the answer, Jason ventured, "You look really familiar. Who are you?"

The man smiled gently again, almost as if he were amused at the entire world. "Jason, my boy, you know who I am. You're simply afraid to admit it."

"Are you my grandpa Moyer?" Jason asked in a hesitant voice, barely above a whisper.

"Yes, Jason, I'm your grandfather. If you like, you can call me James. If that seems too formal, feel free to call me Jim if that's more comfortable. After all, we never had the chance to get to know each other and it seems this may be as good a time as any to correct that particular deficiency."

His head swimming with the implications, and no less than a thousand unanswered questions, Jason asked, "Wouldn't you rather have me call you Grandpa?"

"I would like that very much, Jason, but I don't want to force a family relationship on you that you may not be comfortable with."

"Comfortable may not be how I would describe my current situation, but I do feel a lot better than I did a few minutes ago." Jason sat quietly for a few moments considering, and then asked, "Grandpa, why are you here?"

Grandpa smiled the same bittersweet smile as before. "Jason, I've been keeping an eye on you for a long time, and in your typical fashion you've cut right to the heart of the matter. You didn't ask how, you simply asked why. Most people would be so concerned about the how, not to mention the what comes next, that they wouldn't even consider the why. But since you asked, I'll tell you. I am here to take care of you."

"Somehow Grandpa, I don't think you're telling me the whole story."

Grandpa chuckled and shook his head. "Jason, the time has come for you to return home. I'm here to look after you and make the way as easy as possible."

Jason looked speculatively at his grandpa, noticing again that in spite of the rain, the man before him seemed to be completely dry. No moisture dampened his blond hair or soaked into his flight jacket. "You are real, aren't you? After all, with the bump I took on my noggin I could be imagining you."

"Yes, Jason, I'm as real as you are."

"When you say it's time to go home, you aren't talking about our place north of town, are you?"

"No, Jason, I'm not talking about your farm."

"What will happen to Mom and Dad? How will they get along without my help? When will I see them again?"

"Slow down young feller," smiled Grandpa. "Time may be a bit short but I think I can answer your questions, at least the most important ones."

Jason nodded and waited expectantly.

Grandpa continued, "Jason, your mother will be fine. She's a strong woman. In fact, almost before you know it you'll be seeing her again."

Jason waited, but when nothing more was forthcoming he asked, "What about Dad?"

"Your dad's a good man. A strong man. In fact, he's a better man than he knows and with a little helpful persuasion he will learn just how good a man he really is."

"When will I see him again?" Jason asked.

"It will be a while. You see, your dad has some things to learn." Grandpa paused and looked speculatively at the battered pickup. "It's not going to be easy for him. Mostly, I think, because he believes he already knows the things he still needs to learn. Unfortunately, while he knows them up here," Grandpa said, pointing to his head, "he doesn't know them here." Grandpa touched the center of his chest.

"What is it that Dad needs to learn?"

"Jason, you remember all of the lessons your dad taught you in the woodshed?"

Jason flashed back to what seemed like countless hours spent in the open-faced woodshed and nodded briefly.

"Well, your dad is about to find out that many of those lessons apply to life, not just to splitting wood. Once he learns those lessons he'll be fine. In fact," Grandpa Moyer said with a gentle smile, "he'll be better than fine."

Jason coughed and a trickle of blood ran out of the corner of his mouth, dripping onto the seat beside him. He was pale and drawn, and even though the pain had gone with the touch of his grandpa's hand, it was becoming ever more difficult to breathe. "Grandpa, it's not going to be long now, is it?"

"No, Jason, it won't be long now."

"Will you be here with me the whole time? I mean, all the way, until I get home?"

"Yes, Jason, I'll be here with you the whole time. I'll take you all the way home. After all, that's why I came."

His breathing was becoming shallower and more labored, and his words were barely more than a whisper. "Grandpa, I wish I could tell Mom and Dad how sorry I am. I really made a mess of Dad's pickup." Jason took a few more shallow breaths, then said, "Most of all I wish I could tell them one more time just how much I love them, and how much I'll miss them ..." Jason's eyes were sparkling with unshed tears and he no longer had enough breath to speak.

Grandpa smiled as he tenderly looked at the grandson he had so recently met. His gaze drifted off to the north for a few moments before returning to his grandson. "Jason, your parents know how much you love them, because they know how much they love you." Grandpa rubbed Jason's shoulder gently. "As for this old pickup, don't fret yourself. I have a feeling the damage may not be as bad as it seems."

Grandpa looked at Jason, noting his pallid color and labored breathing. "It won't be long at all now, Jason. We'll be on our way almost before you know it. For now, just close your eyes and rest. I've a bit of cleaning up to do before we go."

As Grandpa Moyer finished speaking, Jason slipped into semi-consciousness. "Jason, my boy, I simply can't bear to have my tender-hearted Emily see you this way." Grandpa passed his hand gently over Jason's lacerated scalp and the discoloration faded. Using his handkerchief, he carefully wiped the fresh blood from his grandson's forehead and face. He straightened the extra bend in his broken arm and rotated his foot so the shattered bones in his leg were less noticeable. Finally, he turned to the truck. He passed his hands over the windshield and the driver's side window and the shattered glass was mended. He placed his right hand on the seat back and countless bloodstains disappeared, into the seat fabric, the floor mat, the windshield glass, even fading into the metal itself.

Leaving the cab, Grandpa Moyer walked methodically around the truck. A tug here, a pull there as tortured metal was put right, and the overstressed suspension was mended. Grandpa did nothing with the damage to the bed where the truck had struck the power pole. The fender and bumper remained crumpled where they rested in contact with the boulder that had finally stopped the runaway pickup truck. He also left the radiator, the broken engine mounts, the shattered fan blade and the lifeless battery. Some wounds Charles was simply going to have to deal with on his own.

Grandpa reached past Jason's battered body and clicked the radio on. The cab was filled with the haunting melody and stirring words of Jud Strunk's *Daisy a Day*. As the song continued, Jason's body visibly relaxed. His head tilted to the side and the unshed tears that had been brimming in his eyes coursed down his cheek, dripping onto the seat beside him. Jason took a breath, and when he exhaled, the only sound was the rain pounding on the roof and Jud Strunk crooning the last verse of his touching love song.

The song ended. Grandpa stepped back from the pickup, extended his hand and said, "It's time to go home, Jason."

As quickly as he came, James Moyer was gone.

The tears on the seat beside Jason disappeared into the fabric without a trace, just as the blood stains had done moments before. The radio fell silent as the headlights and dome light were extinguished.

In the distance, the Utah Power and Light repair truck could be seen approaching the Goshen substation. It was going to be a long night for the repair crews.

The house was dark except for the illumination from the frequent flashes of lightning. Rain drummed on the roof and gushed along the rain gutters and downspouts, flowing into the gardens and onto the lawns surrounding the home. Inside, Charles Jason Tucker sat quietly in the brooding darkness. The cuckoo clock on the wall chimed twice and was silent.

Charles raised his head and considered the dark night. When Jason had asked if he could use the pickup to take a date to the Harvest Ball, Charles had been secretly pleased. He was not entirely happy about Jason dating at 15 but that particular problem had worked itself out when Jason had informed his father that he would be attending the dance stag. Bottom line, Jason generally worked hard, just like his father did, and there seemed to be precious little to show for their efforts. That was the real reason Charles had been willing to grant Jason's request to go to the Harvest Ball. The dance was sponsored by the FFA Chapter in the school and it was the one time each year when the farm lads could strut their stuff.

Charles had suspected Jason would wind up fooling around with some of his friends and that he might miss his appointed curfew. However, he had never suspected Jason would be a full hour late. Jason had proven on more than one occasion that he stood behind his word and could be trusted. *I guess it just goes to show that even the best of intentions mean little when a bunch of boys get together. Still, I expected better of Jason. I guess I will have to come up with a suitable punishment to drive the point home.*

Charles could feel the pull of exhaustion. He'd been up since before four thirty the previous morning in order to milk the cows. He'd then worked hard all day before milking again that evening. In fact, he'd finished up the last of the chores himself so Jason could get ready for the dance. Now Jason was late, and in less than two and a half hours Charles would have to be up to start a new day.

No matter what, seven days a week, three hundred and sixty-five days a year, the cows had to be milked, fed, and bedded down. The work was endless and it took an 'all hands on deck' effort to even come close to keeping up with everything that had to be done to run a successful dairy operation.

Dang that boy, I really thought he was more responsible than this!

Charles adjusted his position in the old rocking chair. His wife, Emily, had retired to bed hours ago, but Charles was dyed-in-the-wool old-school. He'd wait up until Jason got home, even if that meant sitting in this butt-breaking rocking chair until morning. *One thing is for certain though, the more punishment my butt takes from this old chair, the more harsh the punishment Jason will receive when he finally drags his tail home.*

Beyond the window, the countryside was covered in darkness as far as Charles could see. He hoped the lousy power company would get the power restored before it came time to milk the cows. He was most decidedly not looking forward to milking 70 head of cows by hand. Especially not if he had to do it all by himself!

Charles was never sure how or when he finally drifted off to sleep, still sitting in that old rocking chair. With all the lightning and thunder, not to mention the uncomfortable chair, it should have been more than enough to keep him awake.

Charles was roused from his fitful sleep by a knock at the door. Rising groggily from his chair, he pressed his fists into the muscles in his lower back, trying in vain to ease the pain that was making it almost impossible to walk. Stumbling his way across the darkened room, the flashing lights of the County Sheriff's car seized his gaze. The fear exploding in his guts drove him instantly to the edge of unreasoning panic, even as a tiny fragment of his mind struggled with the realization that he might have just enjoyed the most restful sleep he would have for many years to come ...

—The Story Continues—

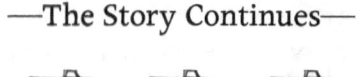

In *Chet: Whispers From the Past ...*

The story continues ...

—Whispers From the Past—

30 years ago Charles Tucker lost everything that made life worth living. A brutal car accident killed his son. A short time later painful cancer took his wife.

The arrival of the Saunders family casts Charles' life into turmoil, tearing open unhealed wounds. Without his help the Saunders' financial troubles threaten to destroy them, but helping them risks destroying everything Charles spent a lifetime building.

Over all the turmoil looms Chet, the battered old '64 Chevy pickup that carried Charles' son to his death. For 29 years Charles blamed the old pickup for his devastating losses, locking Chet away in an old barn.

The most intriguing mysteries refuse to stay locked up. Solving this one promises an enchanting adventure for the whole family.

Publisher's Note

If you've enjoyed this book, please consider signing up for the author's mailing list. Fans who sign up will receive an email notification as each new book in the Chet series is released. We'll also alert you when Larry Murray releases any new fiction titles outside of the Chet universe. You can sign up for this free service at larrycmurray.com/sign-up.

Author's Notes

I really hope you've enjoyed *Chet: From Out of Nowhere*, the prequel novella in the Chet universe. After writing the first three novels in the Chet universe, I finally admitted my fans were right and I had to face up to the question of how Chet came into Charles' life. I'd already dealt with his creation in the prologue of *Whispers From the Past*, but we had no idea how the now-mystical truck joined the Tucker family in the first place.

Pushing the story back in time, the one thing I was certain of was that Charles was not the same person before the accident that took his only son's life, or the subsequent loss of his bride, Emily. I was pretty sure he was a bit of a hothead, with more than a few rough edges. What surprised me most was how easily he was manipulated into the race that ultimately resulted in him bringing Chet home. The seasoned Charles would have never fallen for such a ploy, but the twenty-nine-year-old Charles had not yet brought his ego under control.

Although the race sequence is fictitious, as with most of the content in the Chet universe, I did my best to keep it plausible. I know from personal experience that the three-speed Chevy C-10 pickups built in the mid sixties were consummate drag trucks. Especially when equipped with a V8, you could leave them in second gear for the entire quarter-mile run. On more than one occasion they beat newer cars and trucks with bigger engines. I'm sure it wasn't the best way to treat either the engine or the transmission, but fortunately both were incredibly durable, a fact the racers and their parents were both very grateful for.

One other issue I'd like to shed some light on is the title of the prequel. Two of my biggest writing challenges, at least from a creative standpoint, are the title and the summary. As much as I might like to hand these tasks off to someone else, I've never been able to convince myself that it's possible to do so.

As I considered potential titles for the prequel, I kept coming back to the obvious theme, that choices have consequences and sometimes those consequences last for a lifetime and beyond. I tried dozens of titles on the theme but nothing felt right. After weeks of struggling with the title, a new thread in the tapestry of the story caught my attention. The more I thought about it, the more I felt it is perhaps just as significant, if admittedly more subtle than the inviolable fact, that consequences follow choices.

My focus was drawn to the reality that preceding many of the most profound choices we face in life, are unforeseen events or circumstances that force us to a decision. Often times these decision points are not only unexpected, but are also urgent in nature, leaving us with little or no time to formulate a response before a choice has to be made. These snap decisions, and responses, reveal a great deal about our fundamental character.

In the story, Calvin Ellis never expected his sales manager's animosity to manifest in the way it did, nor at a moment when he felt quite so vulnerable. There was no way to prepare for the heart attack that disabled his customer and aborted the delivery of the sale he had made weeks before. His choice of response had significant implications not only in his own life, but for Charles as well.

Charles is revealed to have a predisposition to hasty, poorly considered, and sometimes hurtful responses to situations that paint him in a less than flattering light. Countering that tendency is Emily's even tempered and loving disposition. Her ability to turn the other cheek, and to continue to love in spite of the hurt, had a profound effect on Charles and the individual he became.

Perhaps the most insightful glimpse into Charles' underlying character is provided when against all odds he is soundly defeated, and Cal graciously offers to cancel the wager. The very traits that compel Charles to live up to his word, are the unbreakable threads that allow him to be tempered, rather than broken, by the trials that await in his future.

It was fascinating as I considered how changing a single choice anywhere along the arc of the story would have taken me as the author, and you as the reader, to an entirely different destination. While obviously true in fiction, I believe the principle applies every bit as much in our real lives. That being the case, it behooves us to safeguard our choices, for with every one, for good or ill, comes a corresponding set of consequences.

Finally, a housekeeping issue. For the reader of the entire Chet series, the epilogue in *From Out of Nowhere*, is the same as the prologue in the ensuing *Whispers From the Past*. I felt the information was critical for completing the story in the novella, so I included it as the epilogue. For any who skip the novella, and start with the first novel, Jason's late night experience is essential context for the rest of the story. For those who read both, you can safely skip the content in one place or the other.

Acknowledgments

It has never been my intent to force my Christian beliefs on others, but they are such a part of me that it's impossible to know me without getting at least a sense of what I believe and how I try to live my life. With that in mind, I recognize from whence all my blessings and talents come and I wish to thank my Father in heaven for all that I am, and for the opportunity to write and hopefully make the world a better place, one story at a time.

Next on my list of those who deserve special thanks is my bride of thirty-nine years. She has put up with more than any woman should have to endure, especially over the past dozen years. Loa, thank you for believing in me, and for standing by me through thick and thin. Your support through all my challenges and self-doubts has made all the difference in the world. I couldn't have done it without you.

Dean, thank you for all the encouragement. The indie publishing road is not the easiest to navigate and I know you've had to talk me down way more often than anyone could rationally expect. Thank you for your mentoring and for blazing so many of the trails I have followed these past few years.

Thank you to my editor, RJ Locksley. The Chet universe is more concise and understandable, in large part because of your guidance. Thank you to my illustrator, Brian Call. Your amazing artwork continues to provide the visual introduction to the star and cast of the stories. Thank you to Katie Murray for your assistance with the cover design.

Thank you to my advance readers, Loa, Dean, Pam, Matthew, Katie, Shalese, and Lachele. This book would not be as good as it is without your suggestions and feedback.

Last, but certainly not least, thank you to each and every person who has read my stories. I hope you have found them worthwhile and enjoyable, and that in some small way they have made your life better.

About the Author

Larry Murray started writing professionally in the '90s, when print was still pretty much the only game in town. His professional life has always followed the technical disciplines, and as a result Larry's creative efforts were largely engaged in nonfiction writing. Over the past twenty years, Larry has published a variety of projects including dozens of articles, numerous technical training courses and both technical and sales copy for hundreds of web pages.

In 2013, Larry decided to push the boundaries of his creative endeavors and he undertook his first serious fiction project. The result of over a year of writing and editing was the creation of the Chet universe, as introduced in *Whispers From the Past*.

If you would like to find out more about Larry and his latest projects, you are invited to visit his blog at larrycmurray.com.

www.ingramcontent.com/pod-product-compliance
Lightning Source LLC
Chambersburg PA
CBHW030540180626
46810CB00005B/1955